SOFTBALL

RULES, TIPS, STRATEGY, AND SAFETY

— ADAM B. HOFSTETTER —

rosen publishing's
rosen central®

New York

For Abby

Published in 2007 by The Rosen Publishing Group, Inc.
29 East 21st Street, New York, NY 10010

First Edition

Library of Congress Cataloging-in-Publication Data

Hofstetter, Adam B.
Softball: rules, tips, strategy, and safety/Adam B. Hofstetter.
    p. cm.—(Sports from coast to coast)
Includes bibliographical references and index.
ISBN-13: 978-1-4042-0996-1
ISBN-10: 1-4042-0996-4 (library binding)
1. Softball—Juvenile literature. I. Title. II. Series.

GV881.15.H64 2006
796.357'8—dc22

                                                      2006016129

Printed in China

CONTENTS

CHAPTER ONE

History of Softball

Softball was originally invented to be played indoors. Early on, the ball was so soft that players did not wear mitts.

Softball made its Olympic debut at the 1996 Summer Games in Atlanta, Georgia. It's probably a safe bet that nobody there thought about Thanksgiving. But if Thanksgiving Day in 1887 had gone a bit differently, softball might not exist.

That day, a group of alumni from Yale and Harvard gathered at the Farragut Boat Club in Chicago, Illinois. They were there to hear the score of a football game being played between the two universities. While celebrating the Yale victory, someone tossed a boxing glove at one of the Harvard folks. He, in turn, picked up a stick and swatted the glove back over the Yale fan's head. George Hancock, a reporter from the Chicago Board of Trade, saw what happened. Inspired by the boxing glove, Hancock imagined a fun, indoor version of baseball that could be played during the cold Chicago winters. Using the boxing glove's strings, he tied it into a ball. That very night, with chalk baselines and a broom handle for a bat, the men played in the first-ever softball game.

Over the next week, Hancock and other members of the Farragut Boat Club wrote up some rules. Hancock developed a ball with a 16-inch (40 centimeter) circumference and a small bat. Because the ball was soft, players did not wear mitts as in baseball. The game quickly spread all over Chicago.

In 1889, Hancock issued the first softball rule book. Hancock's game wasn't called soft-ball just yet. It was simply called indoor baseball. When the game achieved national popularity in the 1890s, it was known as kitten league ball or kitten ball, named after one of the first teams to play it.

In 1895, a fireman named Lewis Rober Sr. from Minneapolis, Minnesota, took the game outdoors. He set up a field in a vacant lot near his firehouse so that his fellow firemen could get some exercise. Rober used a 12-inch (30 cm) ball, which eventually became the standard worldwide.

George Hancock (*above*) is known as the father of softball. He invented the game and wrote its first rule book.

Over the years, the game was also called diamond ball, pumpkin ball, and mush ball. Finally, in 1926, Walter Hakanson of the YMCA of Denver, Colorado, called the game softball when he suggested it to the International Joint Rules Committee.

Softball's Popularity Spreads

Like the ball, the game's rules also took a long time to be standardized. Softball leagues were springing up quickly, and each one fashioned its own set of rules to fit the players and the circumstances. Some leagues preferred the fast-pitch game, while others preferred slow-pitch softball. Some groups allowed teams to use a tenth fielder, while others followed traditional baseball rules and allowed only nine fielders. What the sport needed was a national governing body to organize teams and direct the growth of the sport.

In 1933, the first national amateur softball tournament was held. Organizers wisely scheduled the tournament as part of the Chicago World's Fair, which helped introduce the game to people from all over the country and the world. Champions were crowned in a women's division and in men's fast-pitch and slow-pitch. The success of the tournament finally led to the founding of the Amateur Softball Association (ASA) later that year. This group produced the first widely accepted rule book. In addition, the ASA went on to organize consistent and fair tournaments around the country. With the rules standardized, the game grew even more rapidly. Historians estimate that as many as five million people around the world were playing organized softball by the end of the 1930s.

During World War II (1941–1945), softball spread internationally, as American soldiers played and taught the game wherever they were stationed. The game took another big leap forward in 1946, with the establishment of the U.S. National Fastball League.

The week of July 22–28, 1951, was declared National Softball Week, and the following year saw the founding of the International Softball Federation (ISF). The ISF is now the governing body for the sport all over the world.

American servicemen stationed overseas during World War II helped spread softball internationally. Those pictured here are playing on a beach in the South Pacific.

Softball Goes Global

In 1965, women's teams from five countries competed in Australia in the game's first world championship. The host team took home the title. The first men's world championship was held in Mexico the following year, with the U.S. men's team prevailing. Softball continued to expand, adding junior men's and junior women's world championships in 1981, and the Men's World Slow Pitch Championship in 1987. By then, tens of millions of people around

The King and His Court

In the spring of 1946, twenty-one-year-old Eddie Feigner was pitching for a local fast-pitch team in Pendleton, Oregon. After walloping yet another opposing team, Feigner was heckled by players from the losing team. In response, he boasted, "I would play you with only my catcher, but you would walk us both." On a dare, the opposing manager challenged Feigner to play against his nine-man squad with only four players: pitcher, catcher, first baseman, and shortstop. Feigner and his three teammates accepted the challenge.

Feigner and his team named themselves the King and His Court. Incredibly, they won their first four-on-nine game by a score of 7–0. Eddie "the King" Feigner pitched a perfect game, striking out nineteen of the twenty-one batters in the seven-inning game.

Before long, Feigner and his team were touring all over the world. The King wowed fans and hitters with a fastball that was once clocked at 104 miles (167 kilometers) per hour. In 1967, in an exhibition at Dodger Stadium, Feigner struck out six baseball legends, including Willie Mays, Brooks Robinson, and Roberto Clemente, all in a row!

Eddie Feigner, pictured here in 1951, was one of the most innovative and successful softball pitchers of all time. Pitching behind his back was just one of his many tricks.

The King and His Court dominated so thoroughly that they started concentrating more on amusing the fans with trick plays and other high jinks. For parts of each game, Feigner would pitch behind his back, between his legs, blindfolded, from second base, or even from center field.

In 2006, at the age of eighty-one, the King finally retired after his sixty-first year of touring the world with his Court.

the world were playing softball in Little Leagues, in weekend pickup games, and in major college athletic programs. Perhaps the biggest advancement in the sport's popularity came in 1996, when women's fast-pitch softball was included at the Summer Olympics, in Atlanta, Georgia. The U.S. women's team won the first Olympic gold medal that year, and the fast-pitch game spiked in popularity and participation. The U.S. Women's National Team won Olympic gold again in both 2000 and 2004. Unfortunately, in July 2005, the International Olympic Committee voted to drop softball (and baseball, too) from the Olympics, beginning with the 2012 Games. Nonetheless, the game will still be included in the 2008 Olympics, and it continues to be played by fans of all ages throughout the world.

The 2004 U.S. Olympic softball team celebrates its gold medal victory over Australia. Several of these Olympic players have gone on to professional softball careers.

CHAPTER TWO

Playing the Game

Softball is for everyone. Players are old and young, male and female, left-handed and right-handed.

All types of people play softball, at all levels of competition. Players at the highest levels are great athletes. However, you don't have to be in top shape to enjoy the game. Boys and girls as young as five or six years old play, as do adults well past retirement age.

Despite its origins as an indoor game, softball is now almost always played outdoors. It can be played year-round in warmer climates, but the season is usually limited to spring and summer in colder areas. (Truly dedicated players may join "frostbite" leagues, which play games well into the fall.)

For an organized game, a softball or baseball field is ideal. For an informal game, however, all you need is a ball, a bat, mitts, four bases, and a large outdoor area. Of course, you'll need other players, too—usually nine or ten to a side.

The Game

Formal softball games consist of seven rounds, called innings. Each inning is separated into the top half and the bottom half. The visiting team gets to bat in the top half of the inning; the home team bats in the bottom half.

Each team continues to bat until its players make three outs. Only the batting team can score. The team with more points, or runs, at the end of seven innings wins the game. Sometimes, the home team is ahead after the visiting team bats in the top half of the final inning. When this is the case, there is no reason for the home team to bat in the bottom half of the inning, so the game is over. If the score is tied after seven full innings, then extra innings may be played until a winner is determined. In extra innings, if the visiting team pulls ahead, the home team gets an opportunity in the bottom of the inning to tie the score or take the lead. If the home team goes ahead in extra innings, it wins the game.

Some slow-pitch softball leagues use a "mercy rule" to end a game that is no longer competitive. For example, if one team is beating the other by ten or twelve runs, the game is called off, and victory is awarded to the team that is far ahead. Usually, the rule is in effect only after the losing team has had at least three or four chances to bat.

The Field

The exact size of a softball field can vary greatly, but the shape is always the same: four bases are set 60 feet (18.3 meters) apart (65 feet [19.8 m] for

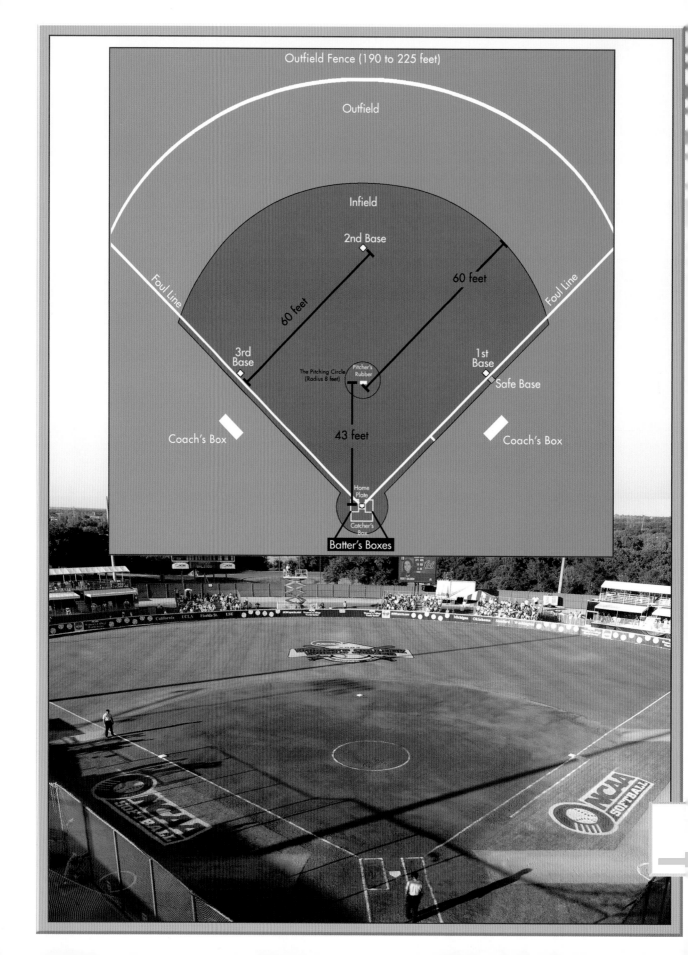

slow-pitch), forming a diamond. Home plate is a five-sided slab of rubber that is 17 inches (43.2 cm) wide. First, second, and third bases are numbered counterclockwise and are each 15 inches (38.1 cm) square. Lines extend from home plate toward first base and from home to third base. Known as foul lines, they extend past the bases into the outfield. They separate fair territory (inside the lines) from foul territory (outside the lines).

For safety reasons, many leagues require a "safe base." This is a first base that is actually two bases, one of which sits in foul territory. To avoid collisions between the runner and the first baseman, the batter runs toward the foul base after hitting the ball. The defensive players use the "regular" base to try to get the runner out. For informal games, though, just about anything can be used for a base, like a backpack or a jacket. That's the infield; the area beyond the bases is known as the outfield. On many fields, a fence marks the outfield boundary.

Other Parts of the Field

Along each foul line, but safely behind it, is a dugout. The dugout is a long, narrow area for team members who are not on the field. At the higher levels of competition, dugouts often include equipment racks, water fountains, and telephones that call other parts of the ballpark. In public parks, dugouts might be just a wooden bench for players to sit on. Behind the dugouts is the area where spectators can sit, whether that is a patch of grass or raised grandstands.

Finally, each team has a bullpen. This is a designated area outside the field of play where backup pitchers can throw practice pitches to get ready in case they are called into the game. Bullpens are usually either somewhere

This diagram (*facing page, top*) shows the layout and dimensions of a typical fast-pitch softball field. A field (*bottom*) sits ready for action in the 2006 NCAA championships.

along the foul lines or beyond the outfield fence. At public parks, there are usually no formal bullpens, so pitchers can warm up anywhere in foul territory that is out of harm's way.

The Team

In many softball leagues, just as in baseball, there are nine defensive players on the field at once. The pitcher plays in the middle of the infield, and a catcher plays behind home plate. There are four other infielders. Near first base is the first baseman, and near third base is the third baseman. On the first-base side of second base is the second baseman, and on the third-base side is the shortstop. Three players patrol the outfield: the left fielder, the center fielder, and the right fielder. Some leagues allow a tenth fielder, who's usually positioned behind second base in the area known as short center field.

Equipment and Uniforms

All defensive players wear oversized, padded leather mitts that have webbing between the first finger and the thumb. The first baseman and catcher wear special mitts that have extra padding and no fingers. The catcher wears additional protection, including a wire mask and a padded chest protector. In fast-pitch leagues, catchers also wear hard plastic shin guards.

For league games, players on the same team all wear matching uniforms, which usually include caps and T-shirts or jerseys, and sometimes include matching pants. For informal games, sweats or other athletic clothing is good, but any comfortable clothes will do.

Catchers are not the only players who wear protective equipment. Some players, like the pitcher shown on the facing page, wear shin guards and knee pads to protect themselves from a variety of possible injuries.

Batters wear protective helmets. All players wear either sneakers or cleats, which are special sneakers that have small spikes on the bottom to give better traction.

Pitching

The pitcher's job is to throw the ball through the strike zone, an imaginary rectangle above home plate. Any pitch passing through the strike zone is considered hittable. The strike zone stretches from side to side above home plate. Exactly where the top and bottom of the strike zone are depends on the batter; it generally goes from the batter's knees up to his or her chest.

Pitching Rules

Whether the game is slow-pitch or fast-pitch, softball pitchers have to throw underhand, releasing the ball below the hip. There are three general types of slow-pitch softball. For regular slow-pitch, which is used in many recreational leagues, pitches must travel in an arc that peaks between 6 and 12 feet (1.8 m–3.7 m). In addition to regular slow-pitch, there are arc-pitch and modified slow-pitch. Arc-pitches must peak higher than 12 feet (3.7 m) above the ground. Modified slow-pitch falls somewhere between slow-pitch and fast-pitch. The pitcher simply tosses the ball to the catcher in an underhand motion without attempting to put much speed or arc on the ball. Some slow-pitchers can aim the ball very precisely. However, there is usually not a lot of strategy involved in the different types of slow pitching: the pitcher is simply trying to throw a hittable ball. Fast-pitch pitchers work very differently.

For fast-pitch softball, the distance between home plate and the pitching rubber is 43 feet (13.2 m). The pitcher must throw the ball from within a circle with an 8-foot (2.4 m) radius. Most fast-pitch pitchers start near the back of the circle and take a step or two toward home plate to give their pitches extra speed. They then whip their throwing arm around in a circular "windmill" motion before releasing the ball toward home plate.

Pitching Strategy

The movements a pitcher makes while pitching are called mechanics. Using proper mechanics helps a fast-pitch pitcher avoid injury while throwing hard. Proper mechanics also allow a pitcher to get power from his or her entire body instead of just the pitching arm. Coaches can often be a big help in learning good mechanics.

Fast-pitch pitchers use different strategies to try to keep the batter from hitting the ball well. Pitch location is key, as pitches thrown to the edges and

A batter's strike zone extends from the knees to the chest. Pitches that pass through the middle of the zone are the easiest to hit. So, pitchers usually aim for the corners.

corners of the strike zone are more difficult to hit. Second, pitch speed is important. The faster a pitch is thrown, the less time the batter has to react and swing or decide not to swing. Finally, varying the pitch selection is key to keeping the batter off-balance. By gripping the ball differently or using different arm motions, the pitcher can pitch at different speeds or make the ball change direction in flight. Some common types of softball pitches are the fastball, change-up, curveball, riseball, and dropball.

Different types of pitchers excel at different aspects of pitching. "Power" pitchers can throw very hard; "control" pitchers have great accuracy; others are especially good at putting a lot of movement on their pitches. In competitive leagues, coaches will sometimes replace one type of pitcher with another at key points in a game to take advantage of a batter's weaknesses. But usually, a coach replaces a pitcher during a game because the pitcher is getting tired or is not pitching effectively.

The pitchers who begin the game are called starting pitchers. Pitchers who specialize in coming into a game that is already in progress are called relief pitchers. Relief pitchers are very rare in slow-pitch softball. However, in college and world championship games, every team has at least one or two relief pitchers.

Softball Offense: Batting

When a batter is up, he or she stands in an area next to home plate called the batter's box—there's one on each side of the plate. Right-handed batters stand in the box on the left side of home plate, and lefties stand on the right side. The batter holds the bat handle with both hands, with his or her dominant (stronger) hand on top.

When a pitch is thrown, the batter decides whether to swing the bat. If the batter doesn't swing, an umpire must decide whether the pitch passed though the strike zone. If it did, the pitch is called a strike. It also counts as a strike if the batter swings at a pitch and misses it completely. Hitting a pitch into foul territory counts as a strike as well. And, as the song says, it's "one, two, three strikes, you're out."

Batting Tips

- Stay loose. Before each pitch, take a deep breath and exhale. Keep your hands relaxed right up to the moment you start your swing. Holding the bat too tightly takes away from your bat speed and control.
- The simplest and most common batting tip is to keep your eye on the ball all the way through your swing. When you hit the ball, you should be looking down the barrel of your bat, watching it make contact with the ball. Taking your eye off the ball may cause you to hit it foul or miss it completely.
- Follow through on your swing. This means continuing your swing, even after you hit the ball. Following through adds power to your swing and also helps prevent injury, especially if you miss the ball.
- Be patient and swing only at good pitches. It sounds simple, but swinging at good pitches may be the most important tip of all. Pitches that are outside the strike zone are difficult to hit. Don't help the opposition by swinging at pitches that would have been called balls.
- Keep your weight balanced on the balls of your feet, not on your heels. This will allow you to make quicker adjustments to the pitch. It will also give you better plate coverage.

This batter properly watches the ball all the way through her swing.

If the pitch did not pass through the strike zone, the umpire calls it a ball. Four balls entitles the batter to a walk, which is a pass to first base.

A batter's main goal is to advance around the bases in order and return to home plate, scoring a run. A batter either reaches base or makes an out, and then the next batter gets a turn. Once on base, the batter becomes a runner. A hit that allows the batter to reach first base is called a single, getting to second base is a double, and to third base is a triple. Balls hit over the outfield fence in fair territory are home runs. An inside-the-park home run is just what it sounds like: a hit that stays in the park but allows the batter to circle the bases.

This high school softball player uses good form as she fields a grounder. Her bare hand is ready to trap the ball in the glove.

Playing Defense: Fielding

Anytime the batter hits the ball, it either goes up into the air (a fly ball) or down onto the ground (a ground ball, or grounder). If a fielder catches a fly ball before it hits the ground, the batter is out. This is the rule even if the fly ball would have landed in foul territory.

The rules for ground balls are a little trickier. Once a fair ball touches the ground, there are two ways to get the batter out. First, a fielder can tag the batter with the ball while the batter is not touching any base. Or, a fielder can touch first base while holding the ball before the batter gets there. The first baseman is usually the one who does that. The main job of the other infielders is to scoop up ground balls and throw them to the first baseman before the batter gets there. Infielders also catch line drives and short fly balls that don't make it to the outfield.

Outfielders catch fly balls for outs. However, for ground balls that get through the infield, it's usually impossible to get the batter out at first base. If the batter tries to advance to second base or beyond, then the outfielders try to throw the ball to the infielder who can tag the batter out. Getting two runners out on one play is called a double play; getting three players out is a triple play, which is very rare.

Catching Flies

Use both hands to catch a pop-up, like the player shown here. This will help you secure the ball.

It takes a lot of practice to judge how far a fly ball will travel and where you need to go to be in position to catch it. The more fly balls you see as a fielder, the better you'll be at judging them, and the quicker you'll be able to get to the right spot. The best way to practice is to have someone throw or hit fly balls to you over and over again.

Many inexperienced players tend to run after fly balls with their arms up in the air. But doing that slows you down and makes it harder to adjust if you need to. You can move a lot faster if you wait until you're in position and then raise your glove for the catch.

Ground Rules

If you can't field a ground ball cleanly, the most important thing you can do is to knock it down and keep it in front of you. This will keep any base runners from advancing further. Proper positioning helps keep the ball from getting past you. Getting your whole body—not just your mitt—directly in the path of the ball puts you in a better position to react if the ball takes a tricky bounce. Outfielders, especially, need to make sure that the ball doesn't get past them. (There's nobody behind them to back them up.) For an outfielder, the best approach is usually to get down on one knee, so that your body will block the ball if it misses your glove.

Infielders are in a much bigger hurry, though. They have to scoop up the ball and throw it to first base before the runner gets there. As an infielder, you should stay on your feet whenever possible, but still try to get your body in front of the ball. You should also make sure to bend your knees, keeping your back straight. This allows you to look straight ahead at the ball instead of down at the ground. For ground balls below your waist, turn your glove so that the fingers point to the ground. Watch the ball all the way, and use your bare hand to secure the ball once it hits your glove.

Fielding a grounder is only the first step. Once you have the ball, set yourself properly to make a strong, accurate throw.

Catch First, Then Throw

One common mistake by fielders in all positions is thinking about what to do with the ball before it's actually in your glove. You can't throw what you don't have, so make sure you watch the ball go into your glove before you try to do anything with it.

Softball and Baseball: What's the Difference?

Softballs and baseballs are constructed the same way. They both have a core made of rubber or rubber and cork. This core is wrapped in layers of tightly wound string or yarn and covered with stitched leather. The main difference is that the yarn in softballs is wound with less tension than a baseball. This means that a softball will not travel as far as a baseball hit with the same force.

A softball (*above, top*) measures 12 inches (30.5 cm) around. A baseball (*bottom*) measures only 9 inches (22.9 cm) around.

In addition to being played with different balls, baseball and softball have different bats. The barrel of a softball bat—the wide part of the bat that strikes the ball—is longer than the barrel of a baseball bat, providing a bigger "sweet spot." The differences in the bats are a direct result of the differences in the ball. Because baseballs can travel farther than softballs, baseball bats are designed to help the batter hit the ball as hard and as far as possible. In softball, on the other hand, hit placement is often more important than distance. So, softball bats are designed to give the hitter better bat control and more command of where the ball goes.

CHAPTER THREE

Rules and Strategy

The basic rules of softball are similar to baseball's rules, with a few key differences. Specific softball rules may change depending on the level of competition.

Umpires

No matter the level of play, the umpires are in charge. Umpires are impartial judges who watch the action on the field, enforce the rules of the game, and have the final say on all questions and disputes. Depending on the league and the level of play, there may be only one umpire or as many as six. And each umpire has a specific job. The home plate umpire calls balls and strikes, standing

Umpires have the final say on everything that happens on the field. This umpire is in excellent position to call the play.

behind the catcher to get the best view of every pitch. Like the catcher, the home plate umpire wears a protective mask and chest pad.

Base umpires stand near the bases and decide whether a runner is safe or out, and call whether a batted ball is fair or foul. If there is only one umpire present, he or she stands behind the pitcher to be able to see as much of the field as possible. Most fast-pitch games are called by a crew of two umpires. One stands behind home plate, calling balls and strikes and foul balls, and the other umpire stands near second base, making most other calls. Umpires are often called by the nickname "Blue" because of the color of most of their uniforms.

Managing and Strategy

Every competitive softball team has a manager; teams may also have coaches. The manager's job varies depending on

Managers and coaches have to know softball strategy. In addition, they need to know how to motivate team members to play to the best of their ability.

Making the Batting Order

The batting order, or lineup, must stay the same throughout the game, so there's a great deal of strategy involved in making it up. In general, the better hitters go toward the top of the batting order. The first batter in the order is called the leadoff hitter. He or she is usually a fast runner who is good at getting on base. Often, the second hitter is also speedy. The team's best hitter usually bats in the third position. The idea is that the first two hitters get on base so that the third hitter can drive them in with a hit. The most powerful hitter usually bats fourth, in the "cleanup" spot. It is so called because the team hopes the fourth hitter will clear all the runners off the bases with a home run. If the first four batters all do their jobs, the score is already 4–0 by the time the fifth batter comes up to the plate. The game rarely works out exactly that way, but this is the most commonly used strategy in setting a batting order.

the level of competition. In general, the position involves giving instruction, organizing team practices, saying who plays the field and when, setting the batting order for each game, and coming up with a game strategy.

The manager also handles all player substitutions. This can be a tricky job because, unlike most other sports, players who come out of a game are not allowed back in. Additionally, a player who is entering the game as a substitution must bat in the same spot in the batting order as the player who was replaced.

Coaches often have a specialty, either pitching or hitting, and they sometimes double as base coaches. Base coaches stand in foul territory outside first and third bases, telling runners when it's safe to run to the next base. They also use hand signals to give advice to batters and base runners. Before each pitch, the third-base coach shows the batter a sequence of hand signs designed to convey secret instructions without letting the other team know what to expect. The coach usually gets those instructions from the manager.

One of the common instructions tells the batter to bunt. For a bunt, the batter attempts to hit the ball gently by simply sticking the bat out in the path of the ball instead of swinging the bat through the strike zone. The goal is to make the ball roll slowly a short distance and then stop, making the fielders run from their normal positions to pick it up. This often gives the batter enough time to reach first base safely. Another reason to bunt is to advance a

Even Olympic softball players are asked to bunt when the situation calls for it. Here, U.S. player Natasha Watley lays one down at the 2004 Games.

runner who is already on base. For these bunts, called sacrifices, the batter is intentionally making an out in order to help his or her team move the runner to the next base.

Baserunning

When a batter hits a ground ball and runs to first base, what happens if another runner is already on first base? That runner has to make room for the

Sliding is an effective way to avoid being tagged out when trying to advance to the next base. Sliding also helps the runner stop on the base instead of accidentally overrunning it.

Stealing and Tagging Up

In fast-pitch softball, a runner may try to advance to the next base at any time. However, because of the risk of being tagged out, the runner usually waits until the batter hits the ball before running for the next base. "Stealing" a base means that the runner tries running to the next base while the pitcher is in the act of pitching the ball. If the runner is not quick enough, the play can backfire. The catcher can throw the ball to the player guarding the next base, who may tag the runner out.

In addition to stealing bases and running on a hit, runners can try to advance after a fly ball has been caught or when a fielder makes an error. Advancing after a fly ball has been caught is called tagging up.

batter by running to second base. He or she is "forced" to run. If another runner is already occupying second base, that runner has to make room by going to third, and so on. The same carousel is set in motion if a batter walks, although all the runners get a pass to the next base.

If there's a runner on second or third base only, and the batter hits a ground ball, the runner on base may advance if it's safe to do so, but he or she is not forced to go.

When a runner is forced to run to the next base by a batter or runner behind him or her, a fielder who is holding the ball may get that runner out by simply touching or stepping on the base the runner is trying to reach, rather than tagging the runner with the ball. That's called a force out. But if there's nobody behind the runner forcing him or her to advance to the next base, then that runner can only be put out with a tag.

The most common type of force play is made at first base. A batter who drives a ball on the ground into fair territory must run to first base. If a defensive player fields the ball and throws it to first base (that is, to a fielder who is touching first base while catching the ball) before the batter can reach it, the batter is out.

When the batter hits a ground ball, runners may move up even if they're not forced, but fly balls work a bit differently. If a runner leaves his or her base before a fly ball is caught, the runner must return to the base. If a fielder with the ball can step on the base before the runner gets back, the runner is out; double play. However, if the runner stays on the base until the fly ball is caught, he or she may remain safely on the base or try to advance.

This runner stretches to reach the "safe base," while the first baseman uses the regular base to try to make the putout. The double base prevents the two players from bumping into each other.

CHAPTER FOUR

Play Ball

Softball equipment is easy to find at any sporting goods store. If you don't live near a store, there are dozens of general sporting goods Web sites, plus several that specialize in gloves, bats, and balls.

Getting the Right Equipment

If you're looking for equipment to get started, the first thing you'll need is a mitt. Players are usually happy to let others use their bats and balls, but they can be protective of their mitts, so you'll probably need your own.

A baseball mitt will be fine, but if you're buying a new mitt, choose one that's made specifically for softball (they're usually labeled). It's also a good idea to decide whether you want to play in the infield or the

To get started in softball, you don't need much more than a good softball mitt. This player is also wearing cleats and a knee brace.

outfield, since the gloves are a bit different for each position. Outfielders' gloves are a little bigger to help them reach for fly balls and to keep those fly balls from bouncing out of the glove. Infielders' gloves are a bit smaller to make it easier to get the ball out quickly. It's best to store your new mitt with a softball tucked inside, to help shape it.

Buying a bat can be confusing, with so many sizes, weights, and different types of aluminum. In general, stronger players should use bigger, heavier bats, and smaller players should use smaller bats. Get a bat made specifically for softball—most softball leagues don't allow baseball bats. For length, a good rule of thumb is to use a bat that comes up to your waist when stood on end. For another way to choose a bat of the right length, use one that reaches just past the far side of home plate when you swing. Keep in mind that softball bats longer than 34 inches (86 cm) are not allowed.

The weight of a bat generally goes down or up in relation to its length, so once you decide on a length, the choices for weight will be limited. Heavier bats provide more power, but lighter bats give you more control and a faster swing, which also helps your power.

There are endless other supplies, from batting gloves to doughnut-shaped bat weights and all sorts of training devices, but a good glove and a good bat will take you a long way.

Get in the Game

Once you have the right equipment, you'll need to get into a game. You might already know of a regular weekend pickup game in your town. If not, you can check out local parks. Another great place to start is your local Little League.

Founded in 1939, Little League organizes baseball and fast-pitch softball teams for boys and girls ages five to eighteen. Local leagues typically have several divisions based mostly on age and partly on skill. Little League has thousands of chapters in the United States, so chances are there's a league not far from where you live.

Babe Ruth League is another option. Depending on what part of the country you live in, they have softball for girls ages five to eighteen, in a league structure very similar to Little League. If neither league has a team nearby, you can contact the leagues' national headquarters to inquire about starting one. Or, you can ask about other local leagues organized through schools or houses of worship. Another option for improving your game is to attend one of the many softball camps and clinics held throughout the United States. These are usually run by former players and coaches.

For young people, Little League softball is a national organization emphasizing fun and fair play over winning.

Play It Safe

One of the first things that any of these organizations will stress is safety. Despite its name, softball can be a dangerous game. Batters and catchers must wear the appropriate protective gear at all times, and players should be careful to check who is around before swinging bats or throwing balls. Even with all the standard protection, softball is a sport like any other, and injuries do happen. The best way to be safe is to do some simple stretching before games and practices to get your muscles loose. During practices and games, stay alert. If you're paying attention to the game, you won't be caught off-guard by a ball or another player flying your way.

Practice Makes Perfect

If you make a team, you can expect to practice on days in between games. At a typical practice for a school or youth league team, one team member will bat while the others play the field, and after a few minutes, the batter heads out to the field and someone else takes a turn at bat. This way, everyone on the team gets a chance to practice hitting, and everyone gets to work on fielding, too. After batting practice, coaches direct fielding and running drills, observing your technique and giving you advice for improving your game.

The Softball Season

As mentioned in chapter 2, softball season is usually limited to spring and summer, unless you live in a climate that allows for outdoor play

Part of a coach's job is to teach players proper technique. In practice, infielders might field dozens of ground balls before they get it right.

Olympic Exit

The 2008 Summer Games in Beijing, China, may be the last time the world sees softball at the Olympics. In July 2005, members of the International Olympic Committee voted to drop baseball and softball from the 2012 Games. In spite of protests from around the world, the IOC confirmed its decision in another vote in February 2006. The sports can still be reinstated for the 2016 Olympics, but few sports have ever made it back into the Olympics after being dumped.

Softball fans all over the world are upset about the snub, most notably International Softball Federation president Don Porter. "The end result is that thousands and thousands of young female athletes effectively have their Olympic dreams fading away," Porter said.

all year round. School leagues and Little League schedules tend to start in early spring and finish by the time school lets out for summer. If you live in an area where the sport is popular, you might be able to find summer youth leagues, too.

At the end of the season, most leagues have a series of play-offs between the top teams to determine a league champion. The top teams are determined simply by who wins more games during the regular season.

Playing to Win

Many leagues and schools have a national play-off system. Little League, for example, has each local league send a team of all-stars to district competition. Winners continue playing for divisional and then regional titles. The American

Light towers illuminate a night game at the 2003 Little League Softball World Series. Alpenrose Field in Portland, Oregon (*above*), has hosted Little League championships since the 1950s.

regional winners and champions from other countries then compete in the nationally televised Little League Softball World Series. This tournament is held every August at Alpenrose Field in Portland, Oregon. In high school leagues, teams that have the best record usually play in a city or county tournament, with the winner moving on to the state and then national championships.

At the college level, the National Collegiate Athletic Association (NCAA) oversees three skill-based divisions, each with its own championship.

School teams in the top division compete to earn a trip to the College Softball World Series.

In Little League and the NCAA, softball is open only to female players, but there are many championships for men as well. A men's world championship for fast-pitch and a separate world championship for slow-pitch are held every year, as are junior men's and women's world championships. Every four years, girls sixteen and younger compete in the Softball World Cup; the next one will be in 2009.

Arizona pitcher Alicia Hollowell delivers in the 2006 NCAA softball championship, held in Oklahoma City. The NCAA Softball World Series is nationally televised by ESPN, a popular sports network.

Softball is popular enough to support women's fast-pitch professional leagues. The top professional league is the National Pro Fastpitch softball league, which drafts college players every year and includes several stars from past Olympic teams. The league has seven teams and a forty-eight-game schedule, and has held a championship game every year since 1997. If you love this game and work hard enough, you just might find yourself trying out for the pros someday.

GLOSSARY

alumni Graduates or former students of a school, college, or university. (The plural form of alumnus.)

amateur In sports, a nonprofessional.

arc An arch or curve, as in the flight of a pitched ball.

bunt A hitting tactic used in baseball and softball. For a bunt, the batter turns to face the pitcher and holds the bat in the path of the ball so that the ball travels only a short distance when hit.

circumference The distance around a circle or sphere.

double play A play in which the defensive team puts out two players from the hitting team.

exhibition A public demonstration or showing.

grandstands Seating for spectators.

heckle To embarrass or annoy with insults or gestures.

high jinks Carefree antics or horseplay.

impartial Treating all equally.

no-hitter A game in which a pitcher pitches an entire game without allowing a single hit by an opposing batter.

perfect game A no-hitter in which a pitcher pitches the entire game without allowing a single batter from the opposing team to reach base by any method, like a walk or error.

pickup game An informal game that can be joined by anyone who happens to be on or near the field at the time.

recreational Done for fun or diversion.

vacant Not occupied or put to use.

FOR MORE INFORMATION

Amateur Softball Association of America (ASA)
2801 NE 50th Street
Oklahoma City, OK 73111
(405) 424-5266
Web site: http://www.softball.org

Babe Ruth League
1770 Brunswick Pike
P.O. Box 5000
Trenton, NJ 08638
(609) 695-1434
Web site: http://www.baberuthleague.org

Independent Softball Association, Chief Executive Office
3601 Cypress Gardens Road, Suite F
Winter Haven, FL 33884
(863) 326-6009
Web site: http://www.isasoftball.com

International Softball Federation
1900 S. Park Road
Plant City, FL 33563
(813) 864-0100
Web site: http://www.internationalsoftball.com

Little League International Baseball and Softball
539 U.S. Route 15 Hwy
P.O. Box 3485
Williamsport, PA 17701-0485

(570) 326-1921
Web site: http://www.littleleague.org

National Collegiate Athletic Association (NCAA)
700 W. Washington Street
P.O. Box 6222
Indianapolis, IN 46206-6222
(317) 917-6222
Web site: http://www.ncaa.org

National Pro Fastpitch (NPF)
4610 S. Ulster Drive, Suite 150
Denver, CO 80237
(303) 290-7494
Web site: http://profastpitch.com

Softball Magazine
411 Magnolia Avenue
Merritt Island, FL 32952-4821
(321) 453-3711
Web site: http://www.softballmag.com

Web Sites

Due to the changing nature of Internet links, Rosen Publishing has developed an online list of Web sites related to the subject of this book. This site is updated regularly. Please use this link to access the list:

http://www.rosenlinks.com/scc/soft

FOR FURTHER READING

Adelson, Bruce. *Softball*. New York, NY: Chelsea House, 2000.

Amateur Softball Association of America. *The Official Rules of Softball*. Chicago, IL: Triumph Books, 1997.

Feigner, Eddie, Anne Marie Feigner, and Doug Lyons. *From an Orphan to a King*. Wayne, MI: Immortal Investments Publishing, 2004.

Garman, Judi. *Softball Skills & Drills*. Champaign, IL: Human Kinetics, 2001.

Oster, Don, and Jacque Hunter. *A Guide for Young Softball Pitchers*. Guilford, CT: The Lyons Press, 2005.

Oster, Don, and Jacque Hunter. *A Young Softball Player's Guide to Hitting, Bunting, and Baserunning*. Guilford, CT: The Lyons Press, 2006.

Potter, Diane L., and Gretchen A. Brockmeyer. *Softball: Steps to Success*. Champaign, IL: Human Kinetics, 1999.

BIBLIOGRAPHY

Bealle, Morris A. *The Softball Story: A Complete, Concise and Entertaining History of America's Greatest Participant and Spectator Sport.* New York, NY: Columbia, 1957.

Dickson, Paul. *The Worth Book of Softball: A Celebration of America's True National Pastime.* New York, NY: Facts on File, 1994.

International Softball Federation. "The History of Softball." Retrieved January 26, 2006 (http://www.internationalsoftball.com/english/the_isf/history_of_softball.asp).

Joseph, Jacqueline. *The Softball Coaching Bible.* Champaign, IL: Human Kinetics, 2002.

The King and His Court. "It All Started on a Dare." 2003. Retrieved February 21, 2006 (http://www.kingandhiscourt.com).

Strahan, Kathy. *Coaching Girls' Softball: From the How-To's of the Game to Practical Real-World Advice.* Roseville, CA: Prima, 2001.

INDEX

About the Author

Adam Hofstetter is a weekly columnist for SportsIllustrated.com. This is Hofstetter's second sports book for Rosen Publishing. He is an avid softball player and can often be found on the various softball fields of New York, where he lives with his wife and two children.

Photo Credits

Cover (top), p. 25 by Donna Binder © The Rosen Publishing Group and Donna Binder; cover (left, right), pp. 9, 17, 21, 37 © Getty Images; cover (field) © Omar Torres/AFP/Getty Images; pp. 1, 3, 19, 22, 28, 30, 32, 34 © Shutterstock; p. 4 Chicago History Museum; p. 5 Photography Collection, Miriam and Ira D. Wallach Division of Art, Prints and Photographs, The New York Public Library, Astor, Lenox and Tilden Foundations; p. 7 © Time & Life Pictures/Getty Images; p. 8 © Hy Peskin/ Time & Life Pictures/Getty Images; p. 10 © Peter Hvizdak/The Image Works; p. 12 (bottom) © Jeffrey Haderthauer/Icon SMI; ; p. 15 © www.istockphoto.com/Bill Grove; p. 20 © Michael J. Doolittle/The Image Works; p. 23 © www.istockphoto.com/ plientje; p. 24 © Kathy McLaughlin/The Image Works; pp. 27, 38 © AP/ Wide World Photos; p. 35 © LWA-Dann Tardif/Corbis; back cover (soccer ball) © www.istockphoto.com/Pekka Jaakkola; back cover (paintball gear) © www.istockphoto.com/Jason Maehl; back cover (football helmet) © www.istockphoto.com/Stefan Klein; back cover (football) © www.istock-photo.com/Buz Zoller; back cover (baseball gear) © www.istockphoto.com/ Charles Silvey; back cover (basketball) © www.istockphoto.com/Dusty Cline.

Designer: Nelson Sá; **Editor:** Christopher Roberts